SNOOPY'S
1, 2, 3

Peanuts® characters created and drawn by Charles M. Schulz

Text by Nancy Hall

Background illustrations by Art and Kim Ellis

A GOLDEN BOOK • NEW YORK

Western Publishing Company, Inc., Racine, Wisconsin 53404

I had no one to play with
And nothing to do,

So I called up a friend
To ask what was new.

He said, "Come and get me,
And please don't delay.

Now pack up your bag,
And we'll go away."

1
one

My **one** friend and I
Were soon joined by two others.

It sure looked to me
Like the **two** birds were brothers.

The **three** hiked behind me
Till we met one more,

And then, as you see,
I was traveling with **four**.

The four got quite tired,
So they stopped to nap,

While I sat and studied
Our route on my map.

But when I had found
The best way to go,
I looked up to see
Five birds in a row.

6
six

Next there were **six**…

7
seven

Then **seven**…

8
eight

Then **eight**.

9
nine

When **nine** came…

10
ten

Then **ten,**
My friend called out, "Wait!"

It was time to go home,
So they left one by one.
The first one to leave
Was the last one to come.

There were **nine,**

And then **eight,**

Then **seven, six, five…**

And then there were **four**.
You never will guess
What next was in store.

Three went to a party
Where **two** birds were wed.
One friend took a picture
From high on my head.

Then off my friend went,
The last of the ten.